THE
Road Runner
MID-MESA MARATHON

By Teddy Slater

Illustrated by John Costanza

A Golden Book · New York

Western Publishing Company, Inc., Racine, Wisconsin 53404

The fleet-footed Road Runner (*Speedus Demonius*) was dashing through the desert. Suddenly he spied a big sign, and he screeched to a stop to see what it said.

That's the race for me, the Road Runner thought. *I can hardly wait for Saturday.*

The ever-hungry Wile E. Coyote (*Appetitus Giganticus*) came skulking through the sand a few minutes later. He spotted the very same sign.

This is the race for me, he thought. *I can hardly wait for Saturday.*

Bright and early Saturday morning, the Road Runner ran to Buzzard's Butte. But there wasn't another bird to be seen at the starting line. The judge explained that the Mid-Mesa Roadrunners Club was for humans only.

The Road Runner was very upset. He didn't even notice that one of the "human" runners had unusually long ears...and suspiciously long teeth!

The judge could see that the Road Runner was truly disappointed. He agreed to let the bird run the marathon just for fun. He gave the Road Runner a special number to wear in the race.

At the stroke of nine o'clock, the race began. The starter shot his pistol, and off went the runners.

The Road Runner quickly took the lead. He looked
back over his right shoulder to make sure no one was
gaining on him.

Had he looked to his left, he would have seen an
interesting sight. One of the racers was running the
wrong way. He was a strange-looking fellow with
unusually long ears...and suspiciously long teeth!

Wile E. Coyote's shortcut put him miles ahead of the runners. That gave him plenty of time to do his dirty work.

And the Road Runner ran on.

But Wile E. Coyote was not about to give up. He had already run more miles than he cared to count. Now that hungry coyote was hungrier than ever—and that made him even wilier than usual. This time, he vowed, he'd catch that tasty bird.

As he waited impatiently atop the cliff, Wile E. Coyote could almost taste that tasty bird.

And the Road Runner ran on.

Still that stubborn coyote would not give up. He had a foolproof plan. He dangled a rope from a cactus. When he heard the Road Runner coming, he hid behind a big rock.

BEEP
BEEP

And the Road Runner ran on.

BEEP!
BEEP!

Old Wile E. Coyote was finally thinking of giving up as
he came to the town of Vulture Valley. But a short way
from the finish line, he had another great idea.

As he came out of the Acme Pet Supply Store, Wile E. Coyote felt sure that his plan could not backfire. He would set a tempting trap, and lure that beeping bird right into the frying pan.

As he waited impatiently behind a boulder, Wile E.
Coyote could almost taste that tasty bird.

And the Road Runner ran on…and on…and across the finish line.

   The Road Runner was the first racer to cross the finish
line. His special prizes were a big box of bird seed and a
T-shirt. When he put on the shirt, everyone cheered.
   The Road Runner beeped his thanks before speeding
off across the desert toward home.